Little, Brown and Company
Time Warner Book Group
1271 Avenue of the Americans, New York, NY 10020
Visit our Web site at www.lb-kids.com
Printed in the United States of America   COM-MO
                    First Edition: September 2005   10 9 8 7 6 5 4 3 2 1
ISBN 0-316-05772-X

ARTHUR
Helps Out

by Marc Brown

LITTLE, BROWN AND COMPANY

New York ∾ Boston

It was Saturday morning, and Arthur wanted to play.
"What should I do first?" he wondered. "See my friends?
Sit in the tree house?"
"Talk to Mom and Dad," said D.W. "They're looking for you."

"There you are," said Dad. "You need to help out around the house today."
"But…" said Arthur.
"The sooner you begin," said Mom, "the sooner you'll be done."

"I don't see what's wrong with my room," Arthur muttered to himself. "I know where everything is. Isn't that what matters?"

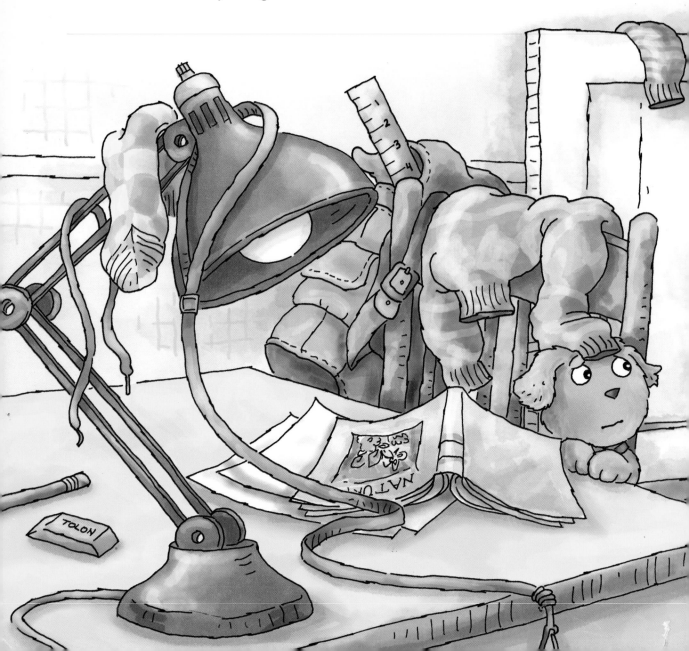

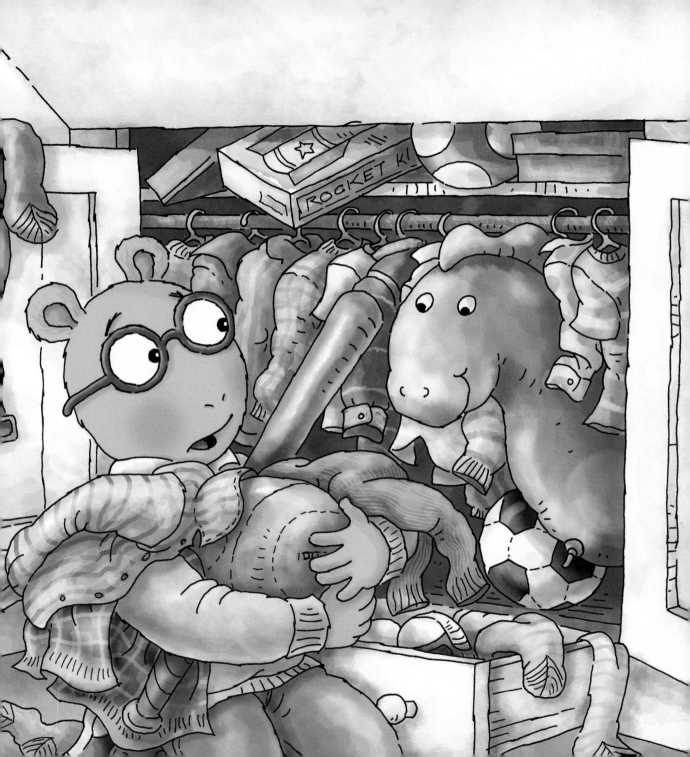

Next, Arthur collected the dirty laundry.
"Don't forget mine," said D.W.
Arthur groaned, "I can't believe you wear so many different things."

Arthur took out the trash and stuffed it in a barrel.
"Uh-oh," he said. His foot was stuck.
Pal helped him get free.

Then Arthur had to give Pal a bath.
"Stay still," he said as Pal squirmed.

Pal splashed and splashed, and Arthur was not sure who got wetter in the end.

When it was time to unload the dishwasher, D.W. wanted to help. Arthur could have done it faster alone, but D.W. wouldn't let him. "Don't drop anything, Arthur," she said. "Plates and glasses are easy to break."

After that, Arthur carried boxes into the attic. He wasn't moving as fast as he had been earlier.

"How many are there?" he asked.

"Just keep going," said Mom. "In my business I collect a lot of papers."

BOOKS

There were still toys to pick up.

"I'll leave Bionic Bunny out," said Arthur, "just in case he has to save the world in a hurry."

"And Mary Moo Cow," said D.W. "That way he'll have company."

"Have you seen Arthur?" asked Dad.

"Arthur, where are you?" Dad called out.
"You don't have to hide," said Mom. "You were a big help today.
But we're all done. Now you can do whatever you want."

But Arthur was already doing just that.